This book belongs to:

_____

To Helen, with many thanks for the inspiration,
and to my dad, who always did my hair just right –A.B.

To Jenny and Rosemary, for teaching me to dance –T. M.

With thanks to Miss Gregory and Miss Webb
at the Jill Stew School of Dance for inviting us to watch
Abbie, Grace, Holly, Madeleine, and Nell's ballet class,
helping to inspire the illustrations for this book

tiger tales
an imprint of ME Media, LLC
5 River Road, Suite 128, Wilton, CT 06897

Published in the United States 2011
Originally published in Great Britain 2009
by Oxford University Press

Text copyright © 2011 Ann Bonwill
Illustrations copyright © 2011 Teresa Murfin

CIP data is available

Hardcover ISBN-13: 978-1-58925-103-8
Hardcover ISBN-10: 1-58925-103-2
Paperback ISBN-13: 978-1-58925-430-5
Paperback ISBN-10: 1-58925-430-9

Printed in China
LPP1210

1 3 5 7 9 10 8 6 4 2

For more insight and activities, visit us at
www.tigertalesbooks.com

Naughty Toes

Follow your feet!

by **Ann Bonwill**

Illustrated by **TERESA MURFIN**

My sister, Belinda, is a ballerina.
I, Chloe, am not.

When we go to Dana's Dance Shop
to pick out our leotards, shoes, and socks,
Belinda picks classic pink and white.

I pick red and purple and green.
"Are you sure?" asks Mom.

"I'm sure," I say.
"It has style," I say.

But the next day in class, I'm not so sure.

Madame Mina
walks around the
room and looks
at our feet.

"Point!"
she says.

"Turn out!"
she says.

"Good toes,"
she says to Belinda.

"Naughty toes,"
she says to me.

Madame Mina claps the beat
while Mr. Tiempo plays the music
on his sunny yellow piano.
"*One* two three, *one* two three."

Somehow I'm always on four.
"Naughty toes!" I hear above the notes of the piano.

Before our next class, Dad does our hair in front of the mirror. He brushes Belinda's hair straight back into a bun, all neat and tidy.

She looks like a swan.

Mine sticks out all over like dandelion fuzz.
Dad sighs a long sigh as he tries to tuck in
the ends.

"Never mind," I say.
"It's unique," I say.

In class we do expressive dance.
"*Sway* like flowers!" says Madame Mina.
"*Flutter* like butterflies!"

It's hard to be a flower when you
need to go to the bathroom.

"*Float* like clouds!"
says Madame Mina,

and I spin around the
room like a dust cloud,

clap like a thundercloud,

whoosh like
a rain cloud . . .

SMACK!
straight into Anthony.

"What were you thinking?" asks Madame Mina.
"I was a cloud with gusto," I say. Before I hang my head,
I think I see Mr. Tiempo smiling.

"Your palms are spotlights," says Madame Mina,
"shining brightly on your face."
I wave mine around so they'll
sparkle on me like a disco ball.

"Chloe!" says Madame Mina in a very loud voice.
"It's jazzy," I say in a very quiet voice.
Mr. Tiempo is definitely smiling now.

After class, Mom takes us out
for ice cream. Belinda orders plain
vanilla and eats it without drips.

I order pink-bubble-gum-swirl and try to
eat it very carefully . . . but somehow it spills.
Maybe I should have chosen the pink leotard, after all.

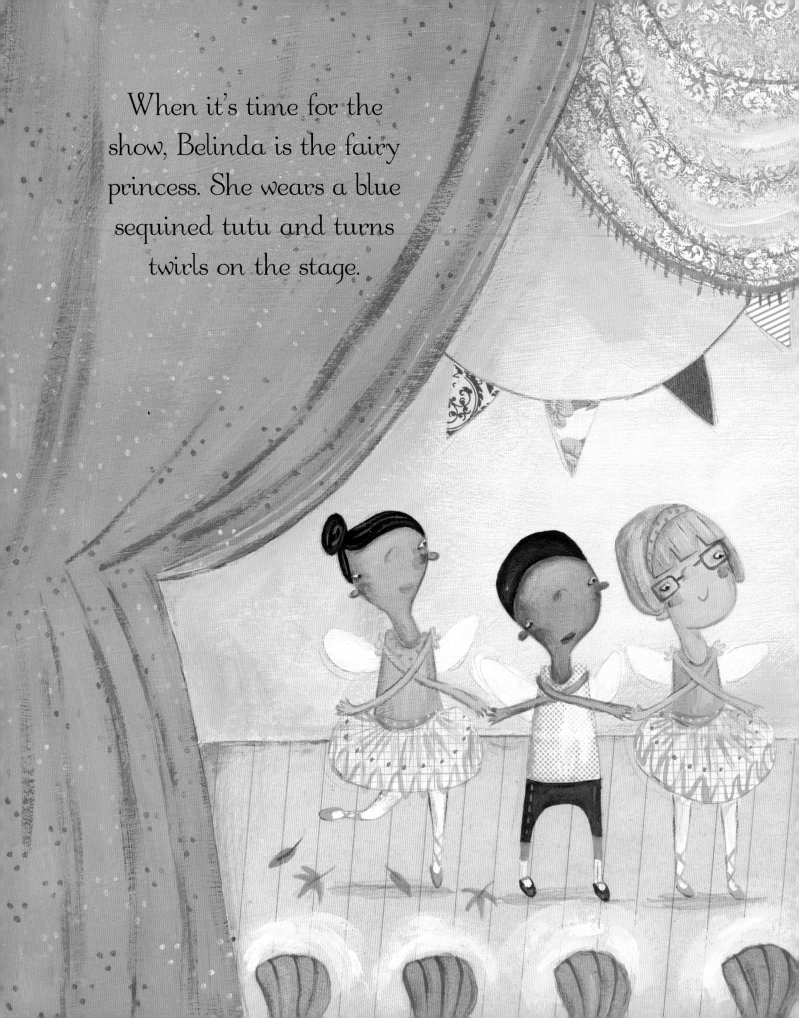

When it's time for the show, Belinda is the fairy princess. She wears a blue sequined tutu and turns twirls on the stage.

I am a rock!

I am all in grey and stand still
on the stage. It is hard to show
spirit when you are a rock.

Afterward we go backstage.
There is a bouquet of pink roses
waiting for Belinda.

It has a note that says,
"For my prima ballerina,
with love from Madame Mina."

For me there is a cardboard box
tied up with red string. It has a
note that says, "Follow your feet!" I peek inside. . . .

My sister, Belinda, is a ballerina.
I, Chloe . . .

am a tap dancer!